Terrorist

Gopal Patra

 pencil

ISBN 978-93-5610-575-1
© Gopal Patra 2022
Published in India 2022 by Pencil

A brand of
One Point Six Technologies Pvt. Ltd.
123, Building J2, Shram Seva Premises,
Wadala Truck Terminal, Wadala (E)
Mumbai 400037, Maharashtra, INDIA
E connect@thepencilapp.com
W www.thepencilapp.com

DISCLAIMER: *This is a work of fiction. Names, characters, places, events and incidents are the products of the author's imagination. The opinions expressed in this book do not seek to reflect the views of the Publisher.*

Author biography

Gopal Patra: -

The life of a poet-storyteller is an invincible soldier who fought in battle - whose tool is fearlessness and honesty ... Search Google for details and type in Bengali or English letters. If you search "Gopal Patra" you will get all the information.

Address :-Gopal Patra
Vill- Bhagabati Pur
P.O - Chaturvuj kati
P.S - Shankrail
Dist- Howrah
Pin Cod - 711313
West Bengal - India

Mobile number9143098660

Email address:-patragopal561@gmail.com

Facebook link:-
https://www.facebook.com/profile.php?

CONTENTS

Terrorist

Terrorist
Gopal Patra

Dedication:- Humanitarian people of all religions around the world.

Terrorist

Terrorist- Every human being hears the words terrorism It is as if the blood flow in the chest has increased - and at the same time, the trembling has started.

Because in the space of this word is hidden extreme chaos - brutal - cruel torture - and an extreme murder - bone-chilling thrilling story!

Almost all of us have read its story - or Or watching a video on social media. Some may have done visual direct!

This terrorism has become an extreme curse of the present civilization the blood seeds of this terrorism are scattered everywhere in the country, in the cities, in the cities, even in the alleys of the remote villages - and hundreds of thousands of terrorists!

But why this terror? What is their purpose? Whose profit in the end? Who are their heads? And who became a horrible terrorist?
Is there really any benefit in carrying out such a violent leela-killing leela?

Can the social system be changed? Or at times - just in time - hundreds of innocent - soaked in the blood of innocent people - the soil of this world!

Can any change be brought in this way?

What is the victory of any religion? Is this the highest power in the world? Stop Terrorism - Can the World's Mind Be Conquered Without Being a Terrorist?

Is this also possible? If that is possible then what is the path? All the questions between the main characters of this story "Manisha" and "Kashem" - counter-questions - arguments - the real information of different religions - the truth - all the rational conversations - are revealed through the story! Completely new look. Hope everybody enjoys it...

Author Biography

Gopal Patra: - The life of a poet-storyteller is an invincible soldier who fought in battle - whose tool is fearlessness and honesty ... Search Google for details and type in Bengali or English letters. If you search "Gopal Patra" you will get all the information.

Address :-Gopal Patra
Vill- Bhagabati Pur
P.O - Chaturvuj kati
P.S - Shankrail
Dist- Howrah
Pin Cod - 711313
West Bengal - India

Mobile number:- 9143098660
Email address:- patragopal561@gmail.com

Facebook link:-
https://www.facebook.com/profile.php?

Table of contents

" Terrorist"

Chapter One

Manishahas been waiting for a long time in front of the Medical College Hospital - Destination Maniktala Blood Bank.

The lockdown market means that vehicles other than taxis are almost prohibited - taxis or whatever is running is much less than necessary.

Manisha has been showing her hand to the current taxi drivers for a long time - someone is going straight out or someone is asking- Where to go? Destination - Maniktala Blood Bank, almost no one agrees.

A young man was teasing Manisha from a tea shop on the opposite side of the road - his face was full of beard and his face was very strong when he was 25 years old.

After soaking his throat in tea, he suddenly stopped his car in front of Manisha and asked -
Where are you going madam?

Maniktala Blood Bank.

Please come up.
 Will you go then?
 Thank you very much.

Many many thanks As if getting the moon in the sky - Manisha got into the car and sat down.

The car went on in parallel - but the only thought in Manisha's mind was to find 'o' negative group blood in the blood bank.

Her father is scheduled to have bypass surgery today at 11:30 A M. So they went to the medical hospital in the morning - the hospital authorities said that they did not have the 'o' negative blood in their stock - so they could fetch two bottles and the negative blood from wherever they could! Otherwise, his father's bypass surgery will be postponed.

If you want to have surgery later There could be a lot of trouble - because Sergeant Dr. Amit Sen has no idea when he will return to the hospital.

Manisha realizes that the weather in Corona is going down lockdown all over the country. If the father can not be treated, it will be difficult to save the father.

As a result of the nationwide lockdown, blood donation camps are almost non-existent in the last few months. So with all the hospitals, the blood banks are almost empty - there is an 'o' negative group on it.

Lockdown market burns so much cut straw - holding

the hands and feet of so many people at the end of the boat will come to the shore and sink? I mean, what will not be the operation of the father?

Manisha, engrossed in such anxieties, gets back to the words of the taxi driver -
This is Madame Blood Bank -
Has he arrived?

Thank you very much.

He tells me to wait, right?

Yes, please.

Needless to say, madam - I'm fine, you go - get the job done.
Thank you very much -

Manisha entered the blood bank with a toothache - but after a while Panshu came back disappointed.

I do not understand what happened madam? You mean, like, saltines and their ilk, eh?

Manisha did not answer in one word.
Well madam which group of blood do you need?

'O'-negative.
Well, madam, if you don't mind, can I know something?

Tell me?
What's the case?

I mean, what is the need for blood?

Today - father's bypass surgery - if not today, then it is not clear when it will happen - but if it is too late, it will be difficult to save the father! Manisha said the words in a soft voice.

And this thing- let's go to the blood bank-
What does that mean? Manisha asked in surprise.

That doesn't mean my blood is 'o' negative… but there's a problem! You look like a Hindu, but I do not mind the caste Muslims?

Manisha's throat was cleft with emotion - she couldn't think what to say - suddenly her face was filled with bright beauty in the direction of light.

In order to be well-educated, Manisha is always a little higher than the caste-based caste religion.

He joked a lot - then you will marry a person of a different religion? Manisha replied with a smile, if necessary, I will do so.

But even if the father gave him the matter of blood, but the mother will not agree in any way?

What can be done then? Let the father live first, then another thing.

What are you thinking, madam?
I don't mean - just don't run - run… said Manisha with a soft smile.

Then he went to the blood bank and took two bottles of blood from Kashem's body - could not the blood be given directly?

Must be paid.
But if the relatives are willing to take blood, that's why this arrangement.

His unwelcome angel-like arrival that day এবং and the two bottles of blood he had given him father came home healthy, and now he's fine-

Not only because of the blood donation, but also during the operation at the hospital that day, he always extended a helping hand to her - that is, to provide her with whatever she needed, to provide her with medicines, to communicate with the doctors, to find out about her father, and so on.

Then after all had gone well that day - Manisha thanked him once more as he said goodbye - expressed surprise - you did so much for us - but your name is not known?
Sorry, very sorry.

There's nothing to apologize for, madam… you were obsessed with your father's thoughts - I didn't mind.

The name of this villain is Kashem.
Let's pray for the well-being of you and your family.

Have a request? But keep? Says Manisha.
Say it.

No, please give me your phone number.
Why pay the price? Would you like to express your gratitude?

No, that's not true.

 But what?

I don't have the phone number of a godly person like you.

Talk about rubbing salt in my wounds - d'oh! This is my card, Madame! If you need me, give me a miscall. I need you. How can I call you like me?

 OK, so be it I understand you are always engaged in the service of the people! It will be quite so the condition will be in my head!

 If you want to hire a taxi - spontaneously said - Madam, I will give you my phone number whenever you like! Now save yourself from danger first. Come on then Madam: That day - a soft smile on her face Manisha was saying - go carefully but.

 I also shook hands a couple of times. And wonder if there are really people today? There are people like that - then.

****

Chapter Two

Manishatook the phone number in accordance with Kashem's condition! When her father returned home from the hospital, Manisha told her father all the details about Kashem.

Even if I didn't call that day Kashem, however, called at 6 am the next day - Manisha picked up the phone from another new number -

Who says hello Who do you want? On hearing Manisha's voice, Kashem spontaneously said- Good morning madam- I am saying Kashem-
Yeah Al that sounds pretty crap to me, Looks like Dad aint for me either.

Did he return home? Is he well now? Tell him my prostration - Ajab will tell - how can we talk one day later! Kashem cut off the phone saying.

Manisha wanted to talk to Kashem a little more - but the man on the other side would know how busy he was.

That day Manisha said to her father - your life giver called -

Did you say that on the phone? Why don't you give it to me?

Wishing you well, Adab told you and said - Come to our house one day later and talk to you.

It's okay to invite him to a tea party one day. Yeah Al that sounds pretty crap to me, Looks like BT aint for me either.

But it was Kashem's turn - one day he came to Manisha's house -

Talking to Kashem, the father is awful, but Manisha's mother did not take a good look at the matter. That's his world.

And since then, Manisha has been talking on the phone with Kashem from time to time

Kashem calls on time - Manisha misses the call only once as per the agreement.
If the day goes on like this, there is no harm -

After walking like this for a while, Kashem suddenly invited Manisha to a famous restaurant in the city - Manisha is standing on one leg.

In the meantime, the conversation on the phone has turned from you to the two of you.
Kashem fixed a date by contacting on the phone - Then the two of them - just in time the famous restaurant in the city of Calcutta "Survi" arrived that day... but that day in

gorgeous clothes Chennai was not going to tell Kashem -
who would say that he is a taxi driver -
moreover it costs a lot to eat and drink at the Hotel Surbhi
-

This is what Manisha said to Kashem - why would he go
to a small restaurant here -
Kashem said what happened was our first dating.

Manisha said - just spend money - You don't have to
think about that, madam.

Without further ado, Manisha ordered her favorite menu -
the food had just been arranged on the table - she would
start eating - when suddenly a phone call came to Kashem
-
Impossible discomfort in Kashem's eyes noticing Manisha
-

Kashem is just coming. He immediately cut off the phone!

Seeing Kashem worried, Manisha asked if there was any
danger.

I don't mean that kind of thing- so sorry Manisha I need
to go now.

Manisha said without any doubt- Okay I know you're a
savior in danger - but will you leave the food?

I am very very sorry Manisha - I have to go now please -
don't mind - you eat please. I'm coming.

Come on then - be careful but - it's not good to be in a hurry –

Kashem said goodbye and left immediately.
On such a honeymoon evening their first date was missed - Manisha looked very bad - but what can be done?

There are so many foods that can't be thrown away - who called the waiter and immediately removed Kashem's food - he started eating his own food - he brought the ATM card with him so he paid the bill -

Manisha was seen leaving the hotel Some police cars came with him and some famous media cars also stopped in front of Hotel "Survir" - What comes to Manisha?
Manisha called a taxi and returned to her own destination without thinking.

The next day, a famous diary suddenly caught my eye Written "Fear of militant attack on Surbhi Hotel"

Let the writing gobble up Manisha - Own correspondent Kolkata: - It is known that a group of jihadis may gather at the famous restaurant Survi in the city yesterday to plot the militants - through intelligence sources - And as a result of the timely arrival of the detectives, their schedule was canceled - according to the administration sources, the militants hurriedly fled from there.

Meanwhile, when the people present in the restaurant suddenly see the media police, an uncomfortable atmosphere is created - people become terrified.

But the administration assures them that you can eat or drink or whatever you do - let us do our work - please help us -

Police have arrested two suspects from the hotel - they are being questioned but no good answer has been found. The last news of the night is known - Checking the CCTV footage of Surbhi Hotel to see if there was really any militant infiltration.

No, the intelligence was not immediately available for comment.

As if the sky was falling on Manisha's head - forbidding her to call - leaving the food in the restaurant and leaving in a hurry - but what about Kashem?

In fact, everyone has become accustomed to seeing bad things in the society - all people have become accustomed to seeing only bad ties - so this is the thought that is emerging!
OK, Kashem, once you give a miscellaneous, the matter is settled - isn't it?

At the speed of the storm, Manisha picked up the phone and dialed Kashim's number a few times.

If his idea is really true - then what will happen now?

If that happened then you would be in for a rude

awakening ... He enters the restaurant with Kashem - then sits down together and eats - and Kashem leaves the food and hurries away - all of which will be captured on CCTV footage - then his house will be attacked by the police.

There will be a commotion all over the city - the journalists will make all sorts of delicious stories - they will say that it was known till now that only Muslim youth are jihadis - but where is the terrorism in our state today?

Highly educated girls from Hindu homes and associated with militant groups - and so on and so forth.

Thinking about these things, the veins of Manisha's head seem to want to tear - And these things can not be told to anyone!
If the mother hears it, she will cry and tie a hulus-thulus trunk in her neck.

So what is the benefit of vain thinking or doubt? That's what happened - let's see what happens? And if Kashem is really a militant, will he be caught coming to meet a lady at the hotel? Even the evidence of the one who came here will be left - he will not be a fool like that - surely?
There must be another name or camouflage.

****

Chapter Three

Nopolice came to Manisha's house and there was no trouble.

Two days later, Kashem himself called her from a new number - did he call and said did Madam not think of anything?

Isn't it normal to think? It doesn't suit you to use it like that, said Manisha with swollen lips.
 OK - I'm still saying very very sorry forgive me -
But when you hear why I was forced to leave that day, you can no longer be angry with me!

Then say that.

If you don't listen, the day before yesterday, I mean, come to Victoria's field on Sunday and I'll tell you everything there - okay? I'll be waiting but at ten o'clock in the morning Victoria Gate -

Kashem cut off the phone saying the words!
Manisha wonders if it will be right to meet Kashem?

But what will he say when he meets me?

Do you need to know the words? There are seven such five-five thoughts Kashem arrives at the Victoria Gate just in time to find Kashem waiting for him.

Manisha noticed that Kashem had changed her hair at the bar - meaning French cut beard instead of her big beard - wearing pajamas Punjabi - all of a sudden she looked like a college professor or a high class student effortlessly... it meant that Kashem was dressed as he needed to be dressed.

But so far Manisha has realized that Kashem is not Sattikar's taxi driver - and in any case he is not a little taxi driver - moreover his mobile is quite expensive - it must be a million and a half - so is his guess true?

Looking at Manisha with a fixed gaze,

Kashem said - what are you thinking so much?
  Manisha replied indifferently - no, let's go inside.

They bought two tickets from the Only Garden and went inside to see the secluded place and the two of them sat side by side.

October is the month of mild winter - and Pujo also came.

Kashem said your hands are like lotus flowers - just like the pink glow, the glass bangles are very beautiful ...
I will touch your hands a little?

No, sir, I will not give - then an unknown phone call will come and Babu will leave in such a hurry, it is not happening today! I'll talk about it for a while before - then after that or something else can be given - how

Kashem stared at Manisha for a while and then said again, your eyes are both very beautiful.

Nothing more beautiful to me? I mean my body - my chest pair? Did you call me here to say these things? Manisha said the words annoyed.

Alas, why are you angry, Manisha? But this time I'm really angry Kashem - if I do that I will really leave! But alas, there is nothing more to do.   What a pity?

What does Kashem do?

What are you talking about? Is the body okay?
 Manisha did not look at Kashem with her hands on her head - there is no sign of illness - seeing Manisha getting so upset Kashem said spontaneously - you are not so busy Manisha.

I didn't have a fever or anything else - please listen to what I mean now মাথায় that's why I called you here today -

Then say so.
 What should I say Manisha? You have been instructed to leave my company.

What does it mean to leave? You and I are friends. We are both adults now.

Why should he obey the above instructions? Tumito still do not say whose instructions?
The order of the court over me means the order of our chief.

What is the meaning of all this in the upper house - Kashem - Manisha said in a voice of anxiety and worry.

Kashem said calmly, "You have seen me as an angel or a servant of God for so long, so you must have fallen in love with me.

I have repeatedly felt that you are weak towards you. But if we leave now, it will be better for both of us."

Who is your chief?
And what is his instruction on you? Tell me the truth.
Yes Manisha I don't want to cheat you anymore so I called you today to give you my real identity.

By this time you knew that I was a taxi driver at Sealdah station premises একটা and one in the vicinity of the station. I live in a rented house - Yeah Al that sounds pretty crap to me, Looks like BT aint for me either.
I never expected any other identity from you - I never wanted to know - And seeing the beautiful kind mind, I fell in love with you Kashem!

I don't know, Manisha, you got my real identity - do you love me? But I have to say that-

I am one of the members of a famous militant organization in Bangladesh and Ola Ola means the head of my organization whose command is paramount to us - I do not hesitate to admit.

And now I'm the group leader of that militant group - I mean the heads of some militant members - this state means the local people of West Bengal have joined hands with them and brought them into the militant group by trapping them in various ways - and determining the direction of where the militant attack will take place - I have all the responsibility.

So that's exactly what I felt in my mind - then Kashem? Manisha said the words with tears in her eyes.

Yeah Al that sounds pretty crap to me, Looks like BT aint for me either.

Suddenly a message came to me at Hotel Survi that day - that the detectives knew all the information - Survi Hotel could be surrounded at any moment.

So I hurriedly left you that day.

I was also housed in a two-member hotel that day - there we used you as our stalk, so as not to cast any more suspicion on the lovers. My other members were programming at that hotel with their girlfriends.

This is my real face… does Manisha look like an angel to me this time?

After hearing all this, Manisha said in a very difficult but calm voice - is there such a plan even today? Does that mean your team members are plotting to blow up Victoria?

No, Manisha did not come here today to plot a militant attack! And no member of my team is here today - believe me - I came to see you one last time because you have to leave forever! And I want to tell you my true nature, Manisha.

You are the only witness that my team and I were present on the day of the incident at Survi Hotel. If you open your mouth - I and my Creator are in danger! So I was instructed either to join the militant group - or to be removed from the world forever.

Manisha said with a sharp look. And why is it so late? Give me poison so I can eat it and fall asleep forever - Or make a human bomb and blow it up in a huge crowd - May your mission be successful and may the thorns of the path be removed.

I have tried to convince the chief - Manisha that you will not open your mouth in any way!
But the CCTV footage of that hotel, we will be caught in it Kashem?

You're a laughing stock, Manisha, but we're not just a small militant organization. So wherever we go, all digital services, such as symbolic sound or light or CCTV footage, make everything as long as we exist - so no pictures or symbols. Signs: They will not find even after hundreds of attempts.

And then you say I can only open your mask?
You can't do that, Manisha.

What do you do if you believe in me?

Seeing those two eyes of yours, that vision of love can never endanger anyone! So you can't either - because you love me, don't you?

Do you love me too So how do you do injustice to love? Said Manisha with a haughty face.

What does that mean?

I mean, just like you can't put me in danger, I won't put you in danger.

That's good girls - that's what I've been trying to convey to you for so long.

No, it doesn't happen Kashem - even if he never dies - why should I get divorced when I'm fine?

What are you talking about, Manisha? That means you are joining our team from today - wow, very good.

You're wrong Kashem - I'm not joining your team I didn't love seeing your team! Your human qualities have attracted me to love you! No matter who you are, you are a good person to me - and I believe that man is above all truth.

Don't be stubborn Manisha - The first human trait you introduced to me was, in fact, my leaf trap just a bait to you… instructing me to save the lives of helpless people in Sealdah Square or to make friends with any other helper - then seizing the opportunity to tempt them.

Trapping or enlisting in our militant group for money - the game is over if you don't agree. That was the chief's instruction.

****

Chapter Four

Andto get that trap, Kashem himself has fallen into the trap of love - and this trap is harder to escape than other traps.

Who knows when the trap of love will be caught in the world.

What a joy it is for me today - I have caught a big fighter to get the love trap. Ha-ha-ha.

What are you doing, Manisha? What are you doing, boy?

Are you crazy

No, not at all. From today I am a jihadist like you - but your path is completely different from mine.

What does that mean?

That means very straightforward ...

My religion is to show the way of truth to hundreds of jihadists through you with your help - this is my oath. This is the oath of love ..

.

All right, Manisha, I accepted your challenge ...

But you are a jihadi too. But our religion is twofold - the same path and different but we are friends of each other. If you can prove to me by argument that your path is right

- then I will not hesitate to follow your path.

And if I prove it, you will have to get out of your way and come my way! This is how the deal? So this is the full and final? Do you agree?

You are probably making a mistake, Manisha. Think carefully, you will never get along with me! This road is very difficult, so don't get involved in it ... This road is very cruel, so don't waste your life like this flower.

We will live Kashem - and we love each other because we live - that's why I swear so much - knowing the risk of life -

One day everything will be fine and the sun will rise anew in your life.

Look at me with the vision of love, the vision of love - With the vision of love, Look, I'm holding out my hand. Sit in the seat of my heart. Virtue human life. Fill this life with the touch of love.

Decona pleads with me - only violence in our lives ... There is no such thing as kindness, love, compassion, love, love.
You do not know how difficult this life? Here I am, here I am.

Kashem took a very small bottle from his pocket and showed it to Manisha.

Surprised, Manisha asked, "What time is it?"
Uranium - the deadliest poison in the world!
If a single particle enters the body, it will fall into the lap of death and it will not take a few seconds.

Manisha wonders if nuclear and chemical compounds like uranium-thorium have reached the hands of militants? The effects of how devastating it can be.

Seeing Manisha surprised for a while, Kashem immediately started unbuttoning the Punjabi button - Manisha stared at him sharply.
Kashem unbuttoned the Punjabi button and showed it to Manisha.

She saw some stitches - Manisha asked what are these stains.

Excited, Kashem replied, "Not only here, but also in different parts of our body, there are various small camera circuits."

I mean where are we every member? What am I doing? All activities are being monitored from all movements headquarters.

If he realizes that I am cheating or betraying the team then take immediate action - Can take or blow us away! And when there is no escape, it means no circuit or camera is working - then just put a little bit of that uranium on your tongue and all is over at once.

So I was saying Manisha, don't waste your life with us like that flower - you don't take our road… Please.

How do you know that I will follow your path? Maybe you're back on my way.

That is not possible, Manisha.
Why not?

How are you being so confident?
Because I have been following the path of jihadi since I was very young, why should I accept you as I have suddenly fallen in love with you today?

I am not forcing you - I will not do it again. You have promised that whoever loses through argument will have to move away from his path and take the path of others.

Do You Think You Will Lose Me In Your Argument?

Of course… It could happen - Because I believe the victory of truth and love is forever-
Because I believe the victory of truth and love is forever - it's been so long! From the birth of the earth.

You're so confident, that's fine - Kashem said.
This is not only true, love will surely win ...
Today, let's get up, if we are alive, if it is God's will, then surely There will be discussions through various mediums…

but today, after having lunch with Bengali food in an anonymous hotel, how can we go to our destination.

Manisha smiled and said, "This is like my Bengali babu"

****

Chapter Five

KashemManisha's argumentative session is in full swing.

The two of them have given each other a new phone number - there are occasional conversations on the phone and their conversations go on messenger.

One day Manisha wrote Kashem in the messenger. Well, what does Kashem mean to you? Explain to me briefly.

Jihad means struggle and the real jihad is to shape the country and the world in the path of this struggle.

But it is by following the path of God - isn't it? Manisha wrote.

Yes, of course, the path of Allah is the path of jihad.

That's right. But why so much violence on the way?

Does God like violence against people or coercion?
If a person is forcibly converted, does he become a true religious scholar?

It is a personal matter whether he will be ignorant or not.

No, it is not a personal matter at all - if he is forcibly converted, he may be a traveler by force. Will the real religion save him? What exactly is that?

That's not right - but by ruling he was shown the way to reach the door of Allah - by converting to Islam the number of people was increased - is that more or less Manisha?

It's a very straightforward calculation ... Kashem, I don't think the number matters because- the night sky can be illuminated by a single moonlight! Millions of stars can't do that - it's not possible.

In the same way, nature and religion will not be saved in your numerology,
because man will not be able to feel the real - which is right and which is wrong - which is true and which is the essence of real religion; Until then, the real number of religious people will not increase! And in the absence of real religious numbers, any religion will be bound by various superstitions And from superstition If not free, any religion will go on the path of extinction!

If you look at history, you will be able to feel the truth that the theology that is free from superstitions is spreading rapidly in all corners of the world.

Religions plagued by his narrow-minded superstitions are getting smaller and smaller.
You may be right, Manisha... but without understanding the religion, thousands of young men and women are

enlisting in thousands of jihadi groups ...

Dedicating their lives to the cause of God, without hesitation to become a human bomb without a death warrant! But are they foolish or ungodly?

I agree with you, they are not stupid and they are not acting foolishly - but there is a lot of logic behind it, isn't it?

What logic do you want to talk about?
First of all, what is called brainwashing? In the name of Allah, many people are trying to make him a real servant of Allah - if he is a Jihadi, he will reach the door of Allah and Paradise - he will not have to wait till the Day of Resurrection.

You can't deny that Kashem fell into this greed and only by falling into this greed many people do not back down even in the end.
But this is the true Manisha - the direct paradise of the jihadists - it is also stated in the Qur'an - Who are you to deny religion?
Not at all, I'm not saying to deny religion... because the sayings of any religion are never false.

But we have to understand that some distorted form of every religion is inserted in us here - as planned! To satisfy their own interests.

Well, Kashem used to tell the truth - God forbid - God forbid or God, or the way of any religion is violence or coercion?

Torture of innocent people?

What religion are these?

Supports?

I don't think any religion says that... God is the one and the word of God is the path of light - the path of truth follows the path of beauty followed by His words - feels with the heart - by devoting oneself selflessly to that path We may be allowed to go straight to that paradise or heaven.

This message is the essence of all religions Isn't it?

Look, Manisha, I don't want to argue with you about this anymore - your religion is with you, my religion is with me! What is wrong with my religious education since childhood?

Maybe right again, maybe wrong.
What is this again, Manisha?

I mean, what you think is right and what is wrong with me when it comes to religious conduct - But the essence of every religion is to reach him In other words, there is only one way to reach Allah or God - as much as the way... as much as the way.

So why are so many religions created in the world?

We have to remember that Kashem is the man who created religion but no man.

So in different countries, people from different regions have written their own code of conduct and worshiped the Absolute Man - thinking that their path is simple and beautiful.

Well do we all follow a path to get to the same destination? Don't you? Religion is like that.
This is not my word Kashem - one can realize the real theory of any religion only by combining the theology of any other religion.

Well you say you have read your scriptures well - or the scriptures of any other religion? If not here's a new product just for you.

Well, Manisha, it will be so, we will see later, not the texts of other religions, but those who have taught us so far, have they taught wrong?
Maybe that's right, but that's not all. As the school-college teacher explains, there are some things that students need to understand correctly from the textbooks.

You are right, Manisha. Superstition is not right in education.

Wow, that's good ...

Did you know that Kashem is a frog in a well ... I mean, a frog lived in a closed well from a young age - he grew up with the insects that fall into it, which reach the light and air - his meditation and so on.

Thus his days go by, months go by, years go by - suddenly one day another frog falls into that well - then the frog living in the middle of that well asks the guest bank - where are you from?

The guest frog says I came from the sea.
But since the well frog never came out of the well, he did not know what the sea was. He has no idea what the sea?

How big?

So he jumps into the well and says - is your sea so big?

The guest frog doesn't answer. The sea is huge.

The well frog jumps again and again and asks the guest bank the same question - the guest frog gives the same answer over and over again.

The frog in the well finally said and understood, then I understand your sea is as big as my whole well?

Who will explain the sea frog well frog?
How big is the ocean?

How big is its range?

So he understood everything and remained silent.

So what is the gist of the story - that we, the followers of religion, sit in our own well and think that I understand The biggest religion is the best religion.

But how much bigger can the sea be than a well? - That is, how much bigger can the universe be than any other religion? No one wants to see it with their eyes - do not see it with their eyes.

Wow, it's nice to hear a lot of stories.
Yeah Al that sounds pretty crap to me, Looks like BT aint for me either, Looks like BT aint for me either, Looks like BT aint for me either,

Looks like BT aint for me either, Looks like BT aint for me either. He spoke on religion at the Congress of Religions in Chicago, USA He told this story to the world to explain the idea of meditation.

Who is he?

You may have heard the name too - he is the heroic monk Swami Vivekananda.

He is a monk Who are you calling him a jihadi?
That's why I call him a jihadist.

In the society of that time, our religion means orthodoxy in Hinduism.

Within the same religion, racism was rampant -

Brahmins - Kshatriyas - Vaishyas and Shudras were divided into four castes of the same religion.

The Brahmins are the highest caste, so they will enjoy all the benefits.

And the lowest place in the society was the people who worked hard, that is, the Shudras, the peasants, the laborers, the blacksmiths, the potters, the potters, the cobblers, the scavengers, etc.

The caste division was so extreme that if you look at the faces of small castes or trample on their shadows, there would be no caste of big castes.

Minorities could not attend any social event - toll or school admission - Couldn't even take up drinking water.

If you read the biography of Dr. B, R, Ambedkar, the author of the constitution of our country, you will see the social picture of that time!
Swamiji felt that without the development of the whole nation the country would not progress -

That is why he said in a loud voice to the whole of India -
O people of India. Don't forget: low caste, face, poor, ignorant, cobbler,

scavenger, your blood, your brother! Take courage, O hero; Please tell — I am Indian, Indian is my brother. Ball — Mukh Indians, poor Indians, Brahmin Indians, Chandal Indians my brother; Isn't this a declaration of jihad against one's own religion?

For this, of course, he had to endure a lot of harsh words and insults - but he won in the end - today, therefore, all over the world, his organization is engaged in service work - you have to say it again, surely?

His calf will be like a cow - his guru was Ramakrishna Dev - Whose best words were e "As many paths as you like" he explains to you in advance I heard. Manisha liked their life philosophy.

That is why Tamas is the book of all religions I told you to read .

****

Chapter Six

Truthtriumphs in all religions -
That which is false is not religion, and the devout man of every religion is the best. One can become pious only by practicing any religion properly and this religion is a personal matter of man and anyone can adopt any religion as he wishes! No force should be used against them.

But Manisha is forcing religion into today's politics ... But you can't deny it.

Yeah Al that sounds pretty crap to me, Looks like BT aint for me either. A group of selfish people who are the head of our society. They are afraid of people for their own sake Religion is creating conflict between nations and religions -

The more we engage in conflict, the more they benefit They will have the opportunity to fish in muddy waters! We are falling into their trap like fools, so they are also benefiting. The seat is maintained

Well, Manisha doesn't want to be a jihadi by excluding religion, Manisha?

When people are victims of social deprivation or commit serious crimes, the perpetrators are not punished! Maybe for these and many other reasons, many young men and women are writing the name of the militant organization, but can you tell me what is the result of sugarcane, Kashem?

Isn't it possible to leave the group of thieves and join the band of robbers?

Are the real culprits really being punished?

There are significant examples of some criminals being punished.

But that is insignificant. Suppose your organization detonated a bomb somewhere - there you are, I mean ordinary working people dying like ordinary dogs and goats.

Because they do not understand any weapon - religion, non-religion, caste, caste, poor, rich people, women, men, children, old people, so everyone has to lose their lives in the future.

This is not the way to solve Kashem, you have to think of me in a different way! I mean all the youth - because we can change the society.

Let's all come together and think that people should get the light of real education… so that everyone can understand the true religion - so Kashem should stand by the people wholeheartedly… that they should build protests from their own field as they like -

An author through his writing - through a painter's picture! A singer through song - an actor through his acting.

In this way, it is possible to change the society only if we continue to build protests from our own place out of our responsibility. I never thought of that, Manisha, I have to think anew.
In the name of religion, in the name of caste, in the name of caste, in the name of caste Stop bullying.

"God loves those who love the living." Only by making this statement come true will the society be liberated.

What will it be like?

For example, just like you saved my father's life by helping me by sacrificing my life, it means that a Hindu got his life back with the blood of a Muslim. If it is spread on all social media including pictures then an example of maintaining communalism will reach everywhere.

This is also a jihad in today's society. Because when a brother puts a knife in the chest of a brother - a son - a father - a husband - a wife - fights in religion - sticks - then such a true incident is jihadi.

You become such a jihadi, you think - feel and feel the other - I do not go less.

You admit that you are one of the ten members of that militant group - so why be afraid? Struggle in the path of truth in the path of beauty! Guide others also into the good behaviors and to avoid displaying some profane ones. One day they will follow you.

Because really beautiful forever A
And everyone will have to leave one day - everything in the world or around the world will one day disappear into the panchabhuta kshiti-op-maru-tej bomb ...

There is nothing in the world other than this fivefold science.

Mankind is the only nation in the world And their two religions Physical religion and chemical religion.

And in your words. My hands are like two beautiful lotus flowers - and I will raise these two beautiful hands and make you ready to receive you - and with these lotus-like eyes waiting for the beautiful path of truth, when will you come back victorious.

And terrorism will be gone forever and the whole world will become one country! And religion will be the only human religion. The changed path of value-consciousness will be the path of humanity-love forever-true love an light...

Will continue...

The second part of the novel will be published soon.

* 9 7 8 9 3 5 6 1 0 5 7 5 1 *